Pretty PATTERNS

Beautiful Patterns to Color!

illustrated by Hannah Davies and Beth Gunnell

LITTLE SIMON

New York London Toronto Sydney New Delhi

The pretty patterns in this book
were colored and completed by:

_____

 LITTLE SIMON

An imprint of Simon & Schuster Children's Publishing Division
1230 Avenue of the Americas, New York, New York 10020
Copyright © 2012 by Buster Books. The material in this book was first published in Great Britain in 2012 by Buster Books,
an imprint of Michael O'Mara Books Limited. It was taken from three titles: *Pretty Patterns*, *Perfect Patterns*, and *Pretty Flowers*.
First Little Simon edition 2013
All rights reserved, including the right of reproduction in whole or in part in any form.
LITTLE SIMON is a registered trademark of Simon & Schuster, Inc., and associated colophon is a trademark of Simon & Schuster, Inc.
For information about special discounts for bulk purchases, please contact Simon & Schuster Special Sales at 1-866-506-1949 or
business@simonandschuster.com.
The Simon & Schuster Speakers Bureau can bring authors to your live event. For more information or to book an event contact the
Simon & Schuster Speakers Bureau at 1-866-248-3049 or visit our website at www.simonspeakers.com.
Manufactured in China 1212 SCP
First Edition 10 9 8 7 6 5 4 3 2 1
ISBN 978-1-4424-5181-0

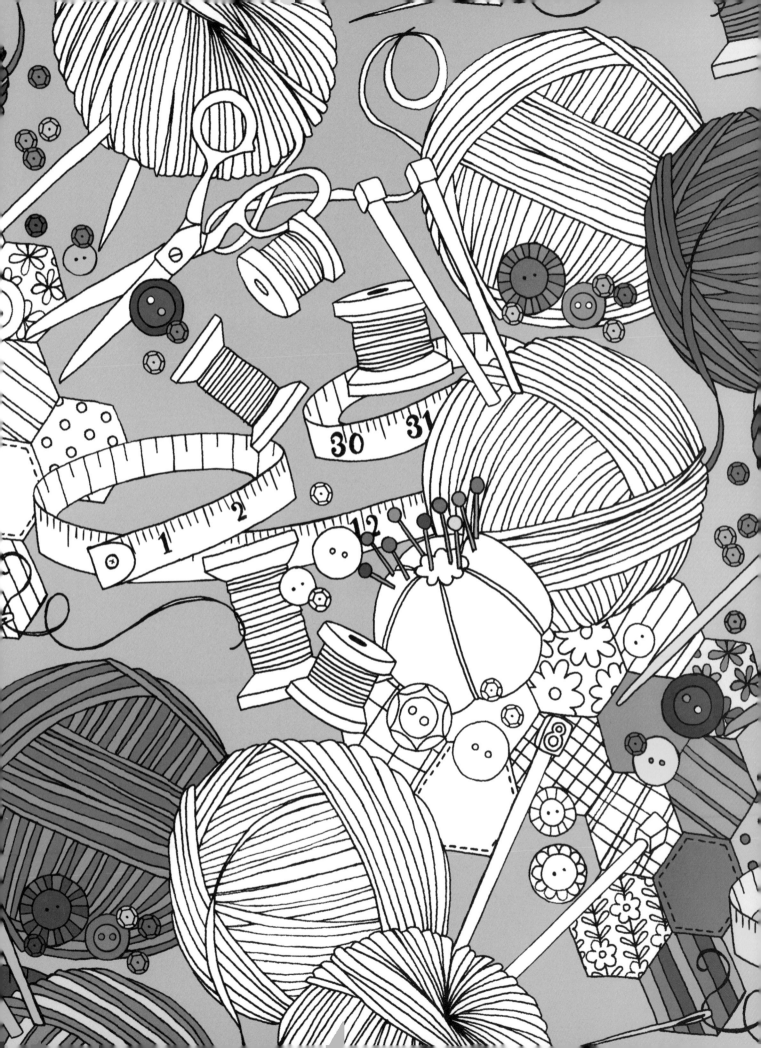